A CHRISTMAS CAROL

Illustrated by
Joe Boddy

Adapted from the story by
Charles Dickens

The Unicorn Publishing House, Inc.
Morris Plains, New Jersey

Old Scrooge didn't care for anyone or anything ~ except, of course, his money.
He simply hated everything ~ but most of all he hated Christmas. And when someone wished him a 'Merry Christmas,' he would only grumble, then shout:

"Bah, humbug! Bah, humbug, I say!"

Scrooge's Nephew

And when kind souls came to ask for money for the poor and homeless, Scrooge would just shake his head and say:

"Are there no prisons? Are there no workhouses?"

"Yes, of course," they would say, "but Mr. Scrooge, it's Christmas!"

"Nonsense! I'll have none of it, do you hear? Now leave me alone. I have work to do!"

Mister Scrooge

The night before Christmas Mr. Scrooge was home alone. But he wasn't alone for long. The sounds of clanking, banging, and moaning rose up through the house.

"What's all that noise about? Can't one eat in peace? Go away! Go away, I say!"

But it didn't.

"Ebenezer, Ebenezer Scrooo-oooge!" a voice cried out, and then a ghost appeared, covered in chains, locks, and cashboxes.

"Marley, my old friend, is that you? . . . Why do you want to haunt me?" said Scrooge, shaking with fright.

"I have come to save you from yourself, Ebenezer!" the ghost cried. "Three Spirits shall visit you this night ~ Three Spirits who will show you the *true* meaning and blessing of Christmas! Beware!" And the ghost vanished.

Marley's Ghost

"Humbug!" said Scrooge. "Ghosts and spirits indeed! Nonsense! I've simply had something bad to eat. A bit of bad cheese, perhaps. That's it. I will be fine in the morning." And Scrooge went off to bed.

"Ding, dong!" the clock tolled one, and the first of the three spirits appeared.

"Ebenezer Scrooge," a soft voice called. "Awake!"

"Who, or *what* are you?" cried the trembling Scrooge.

"I am the Ghost of Christmas Past," said the Spirit. "Come, I have much to show you this night."

"I'd rather not. Thank you, just the same. You see, I need my sleep and I've eaten some bad cheese and uh. . ."

"Come!"

Christmas Past

"Where are we, Spirit? This is not my room."

"Don't you know?" said the Spirit. "Have you forgotten your childhood, Ebenezer?"

"Why, this is my old schoolhouse," Scrooge said, "and the child there, can that *really* be me?"

"Yes, Ebenezer. That lonely little child is you. You spent many a Christmas alone. Without friends. Without family. Ah, you were an unhappy boy!" Scrooge broke and wept.

As Scrooge wept, the sounds of music and laughter began to fill his ears. He looked up to find himself at a grand Christmas party.

"Fezziwig! My old boss!" Scrooge cried with joy.

"Yes," said the Spirit. "He was one that *truly* understood the joy of Christmas. Why did you not learn from him?"

Mister Scrooge

"Money-that became your only joy," said the Spirit. "And your only love, Ebenezer."

And Scrooge saw himself young and strong again. And beside him was . . .

"Belle," Scrooge said with a sigh. "I had almost forgotten how beautiful she was."

"You were to marry her, remember?" the Spirit said. "But gold was more important to you, Ebenezer. Look now at the tear-filled eyes you turned away from so long ago."

"No! No! Spirit, take me away! Forgive me, Belle, forgive," and Scrooge hid his face in his hands. When he looked up again, the Spirit was gone, and he found himself back in his room.

Christmas Past

"I must hide! Oh dear, before the next ghost comes!"

"Ebenezer! Ebenezer Scrooge!" a thunderous voice called.

"Ah!" cried Scrooge, as he turned to see a beautiful Spirit sitting upon a feast of food, gold, and presents.

"Come closer, and know me better, man!" the spirit roared. "I am the Ghost of Christmas Present. You have never seen the like of me before!"

"Never!" Scrooge cried.

"Touch my robe, then, that you may learn of me."

"Spirit, take me where you will. I am *beginning* to see I have a great deal to learn this night!"

Christmas Present

"Who's little house is this?" Scrooge asked.

"Why, this is the house of your clerk, Bob Cratchit."

"Bob Cratchit? Why am I here, Spirit?" In reply, the Spirit simply pointed to the door. There in the doorway was Bob Cratchit with his son, Tiny Tim, high upon his shoulder.

"Merry Christmas!" Bob called to his family.

"And a 'Merry Christmas' to you, Bob Cratchit," his wife said, giving him a hug. "And how did our Tiny Tim behave in church today?"

"A perfect angel, my dear, a perfect angel," Bob said. "You know, I believe he's getting stronger every day."

"Yes, of course he is," Mrs. Cratchit said, holding back a tear as she watched her little Tim hobble over to his stool.

Bob Cratchit

"I didn't know of the sick child," Scrooge said.

"Would you have cared if you did, Ebenezer?" the Spirit asked. Scrooge hung his head in shame.

"A toast!" Bob Cratchit cried, as the family gathered round. "To Mr. Scrooge. The Founder of the Feast."

"The Founder of the Feast, indeed!" his wife cried. "That old Skinflint cares not one bit for you or for Christmas!"

"Please, my dear, it's Christmas," he begged. "Now, a Merry Christmas to us all, my dears. God bless us!" And the family all joined in.

"God bless us every one!" said Tiny Tim, the last of all.

"Spirit," said Scrooge, "tell me if Tiny Tim will live."

"I see an empty stool and a crutch carefully preserved in one corner. If these shadows remain unchanged, the child will die."

Tiny Tim

"No, kind Spirit," Scrooge begged, "don't let the boy die."

"It is not by my kindness that he would live, but by yours, Ebenezer. If you *truly* care. Come now, I have more to show you."

Scrooge suddenly found himself at his nephew's Christmas party. The party he had said "humbug" to, when the happy youth had tried so hard to invite him.

"Uncle said that Christmas was a *humbug*, as I live!" Scrooge's nephew cried. "And he believed it too!" Everyone at the party broke out laughing.

"Well, a Merry Christmas and a Happy New Year to the old man, though I doubt he'll have either. To Uncle Scrooge!" the nephew cried, raising his glass in a toast.

"He's a good lad, my nephew!" Scrooge said with affection. "And I . . . I never told him so. Oh, what a fool I am!"

Scrooge's Nephew

Scrooge and the Spirit traveled to many homes, both of the rich and of the poor, to see the love and joy that the Christmas Spirit brought to every home that knew Him.

"My time is almost done," the Spirit said.

"Please, tell me Spirit, before you leave, what is that I see moving beneath your robe?" And the Spirit opened his robe to reveal two small children, clinging to his legs. There was a boy and a girl. Both were ragged, wolfish, and scowling.

"Spirit! Are they yours?"

"They are Man's," the Spirit said sadly. "This boy is *Ignorance*. This girl is *Want*. Beware them both, but most of all beware this boy."

"Have they no place to turn, no hope?" Scrooge cried.

"Are there no prisons? No workhouses?" the Spirit said, mocking Scrooge with his own words. Then he was gone.

Christmas Present

Scrooge stood trembling in the new-fallen snow. He shivered even more when he remembered what old Marley had said: Three Spirits would visit this night ~ Three. Scrooge turned to look about him, and . . .

"Oh, no!" cried Scrooge, and he fell on one knee before a dark and gloomy Spirit.

"Are you the Ghost of Christmas Yet to Come?" Scrooge asked. But the Spirit said nothing, only nodding in reply. "Ghost of the Future!" Scrooge cried, "I fear you more than any Spirit I have seen. Will you not speak to me?"

But the Spirit again said nothing. It fixed its ghostly eyes upon Scrooge, then pointed a bony finger toward the mist.

"Very well, Spirit," moaned Scrooge. "Lead on. Lead on!"

Christmas Future

"And now undo *my* bundle, Joe," said a raggedy old woman.

"I hope he didn't die of anything catching? Eh?" said the fat merchant, with a chuckle. "Now, what do we have here? What? His Bed Curtains! Lucy, you didn't take these, rings and all, with him lying there?"

"Oh, that I did!" said the old woman. "And his good shirt too! Why, they were going to bury him in it! Such a waste! What will you give for the lot, Joe?"

"Don't worry, Lucy," the merchant said. "I'll give you a fair price. Why, the old man had more friends in death than he ever had in life, eh?" And they all broke out laughing.

"Dark Spirit," Scrooge said, "are those my things lying there? Am I the unhappy soul who has died friendless?"

But the Spirit said nothing.

Mister Scrooge

Scrooge had only to blink when next he saw what he dreaded most: the empty stool and the little crutch of Tiny Tim.

"Oh, no, Spirit, no," Scrooge cried. "Tell me it isn't so! Not Tiny Tim! He is so young ~ so kind a soul!"

But *again* the Spirit said nothing.

Scrooge began to weep. When he raised his head, he found he was in a graveyard. The Spirit pointed to a tombstone.

Tiny Tim

"Tell me, Spirit: are these the shadows of things that Will be, or are they shadows of things that May be, only?"

Still the Spirit pointed to the stone. Scrooge drew close. There on the headstone read, *EBENEZER SCROOGE*.

"No, Spirit! I am changed! I *will* be a better man! Please! No, no, no!" And Scrooge woke suddenly to find he was in his own bed! And it was Christmas! The Spirits had done their work all in one night! Scrooge ran out into the street in his bedclothes, crying:

"It's Christmas! Merry Christmas!" Then, spotting a boy who was passing by, he called: "Boy! Hurry! Go down the street and buy the big turkey that hangs in the butcher's shop!"

"The one as *big* as me?!"

"Yes, yes, my lad. What a delightful boy! Heh, heh! Oh, bless you Spirits, bless you! Merry, merry Christmas!"

Mister Scrooge

Scrooge had the turkey sent to Bob Cratchit, and then dressed for his nephew's party.

His nephew was overjoyed when his uncle arrived.

"I've been a fool, my boy," Scrooge said. "Will you still have an old man at your wonderful party?"

And his nephew hugged him, and said: "A Merry Christmas to you, Uncle, a very Merry Christmas, indeed."

And Uncle Scrooge danced the day away with his lovely niece. Why, he was the life of the party!

Scrooge's Nephew

And Scrooge proved he was better than his word. He did many good deeds, and to Tiny Tim, who did NOT die, he was a second father.

Scrooge never saw the Spirits again, but it was always said of him, that he knew how to bring the joy of Christmas better than any man alive.

May that *truly* be said of us, and all of us! And so, as Tiny Tim said:

~ GOD BLESS US, EVERY ONE! ~

Tiny Tim

Printing History 15 14 13 12 11 10 9 8 7 6 5 4 3 2

Library of Congress Cataloging-in-Publication Data

A Christmas Carol / illustrated by Joe Boddy ; adapted from a story by Charles
Dickens.
    p. cm. -- (Through the Magic Window)
    Summary: An adaptation of the classic Christmas story featuring animals as the
main characters.
    [1. Christmas--Fiction. 2. Ghosts--Fiction. 3. Animals--Fiction. 4.England--
Fiction.] I. Boddy, Joe, ill. II. Dickens, Charles, 1812-1870. Christmas Carol. III.
Series.
    PZ7.C4534 1991   91-9054
    [E]--dc20   CIP
                                                               AC

This book is dedicated
to my wife, Marlys.

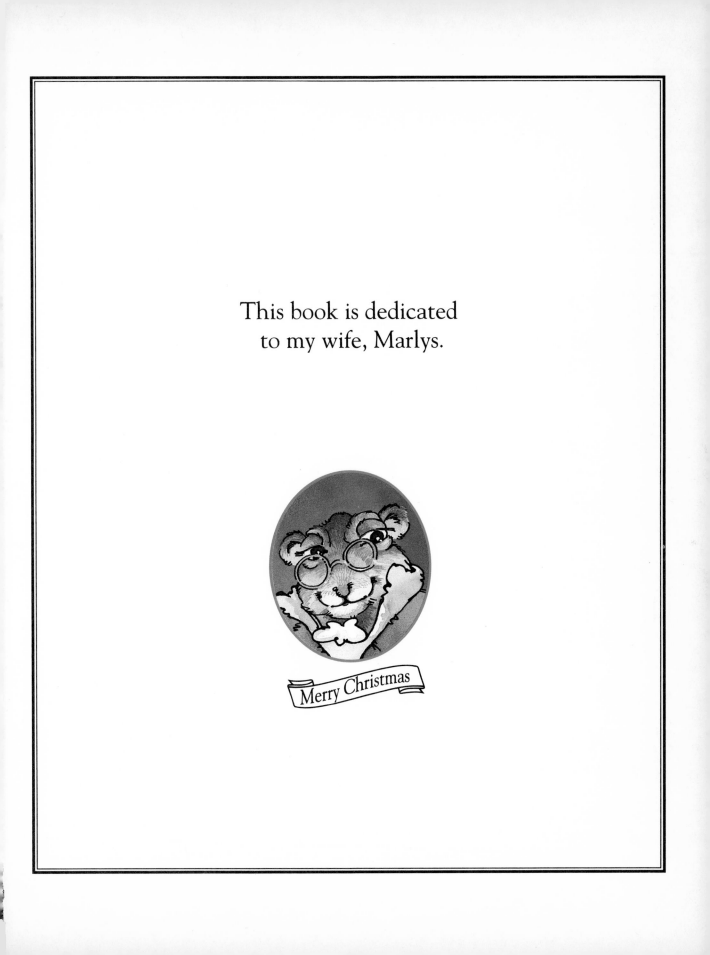

Merry Christmas